VALUES

# THE TOWN MAKEOVER

## NOAH LEARNS ABOUT PRIDE

WRITTEN BY DEBORAH CHANCELLOR

ILLUSTRATED BY ELIF BALTA PARKS

W

**FRANKLIN WATTS**

LONDON•SYDNEY

"Hey Presto!" said Noah, waving his wand. He really loved magic tricks.

Noah wanted to have a magic show on TV, just like his hero, Ali Kazam.

Noah never missed 'Ali Kazam's Magic Show'. It was the best thing on TV.

Then one Sunday evening,
Mum had great news.
"Ali Kazam is coming to
visit our town!" she said.

Noah couldn't believe his ears. "This town's too dull for Ali Kazam!" he said.

"Well, he's going to open the new theatre," Mum said. "He'll be here this weekend!"

The next day was Monday. Noah told his friends about the magician's visit.

They were all fans of Ali Kazam. "This town needs a makeover before he arrives," they said.

On Tuesday, Noah and his friends got to work.
Their parents helped them pick up litter.

12

"Wow!" said Noah when they had finished.
The town had never looked neater.

13

On Wednesday, there was more to do. They tidied their gardens and painted the fences.

"Wow!" said Noah when they had finished.
The town had never looked smarter.

15

On Thursday, they decorated the theatre with balloons.
"We must welcome Ali Kazam!" said Noah.

"Wow!" said Noah when they had finished.
The town had never looked better.

17

"Let's have a party for Ali Kazam!"
said Noah. So on Friday, they
cooked lots of cakes.

"Wow!" said Noah when they had finished.
He'd never seen such tasty food.

On Saturday morning,
Noah jumped out of bed.
"I can't wait to meet Ali
Kazam!" he said.

But Mum had bad news.
"I'm afraid Ali cancelled
his visit," she said.

Noah was upset. The town had worked so hard, and Noah didn't want to call off the party.

"We can have fun without Ali Kazam," Noah said. "We don't need a magician to be proud of our town."

So the party went ahead, and everyone had a fantastic time. But then there was a bang and a puff of smoke...

Ali Kazam had come after all!
"I couldn't stay away," he said.
"Your town is just amazing!"

- Can you tell the story of the magician's visit?

- Why did Noah and his friends give their town a makeover?

- How does Noah feel about his town at the end of the story? Why?

**3.**

**4.**

**5.**

**6.**

# A note about sharing this book

The 'British Values' series provides a starting point for further discussion on universal principles in society, such as tolerance and respect. The values and ethics considered in each book are relevant to all, children and adults alike.

## The Town Makeover

This story explores, in a familiar context, some issues surrounding civic pride. It demonstrates key concepts, such as the value of getting involved in our local community and taking pride in places where we live and work. If we don't take care of our local area, it will not be such a good place to live. The idea of working together for a common cause is explored in the book, encouraging the reader to conclude that a communal living space can be transformed if people work together to improve it. This is also true, on a wider scale, of our response to the global environment. This is an important lesson for all.

## Wordless storyboard

The wordless storyboard on pages 26 and 27 gives the opportunity to practise speaking and listening skills. Children are encouraged to tell the story illustrated in the panels: Noah is excited to learn his favourite TV star is coming to visit his town, but he is worried his town is too boring for the celebrity magician. He gets his friends together to give the town a makeover; they sweep the streets, paint fences, tidy the gardens and get the town ready for a welcome party. The celebrity cancels his visit, but by then, Noah's view of the town has changed. He is proud of where he lives, and wants the party to go ahead to celebrate this. In a surprise twist, the magician turns up after all.

## How to use the book

The story is designed for adults to share with either an individual child or a group of children, and as a starting point for discussion. The book provides visual support to build confidence in children who are starting to read on their own. The story introduces vocabulary that is relevant to the theme of civic pride, such as: 'makeover', 'dull', 'litter', 'tidied', 'painted', 'smarter', 'welcome', 'proud'. To emphasise the improvements made by the group of friends during the town makeover, there is repetition of the following sentence: "Wow!' said Noah when they had finished.' To add momentum to the pace of improvements leading up to the expected visit, the days of the week are repeated in order. This reinforces key basic vocabulary.

**Before reading the story**
Pick a time to read when you and the children are relaxed and can take time to share the story together. Before you start reading, look at the illustrations and talk about what the book may be about.

## After reading, talk about the book with the children:

- What was the story about? Why is Noah surprised that his hero is coming to visit his hometown? How do Noah's friends get ready for the special visit? How does Noah feel when the visit is cancelled? What do Noah and his friends learn from working together to clean up the town?
- Invite the children to talk about a time when they had to work together with other people to prepare for something special. Was it fun? Did they enjoy working in a group, and did they feel proud of the result?
- Talk a bit more about getting involved and taking pride in the place where you live, work or play. What does this mean and why is it important? What can the children do to take pride in their local school or community?
- Talk about different kinds of shared spaces in a community, such as parks, schools and streets. What can we do to look after them and encourage other people to do the same?
- The issue of civic, or community, pride is dealt with in this story. Ask the children what would happen if nobody cared about the place where they live and work. Why would this matter? How would it make them feel?
- Look at the end of the story again. At first, Noah thinks his hometown is too boring for his hero to come and visit, but by the end of the story, he is proud of his town. He realises the town doesn't need an exciting visitor to be a fun place to live. Why does Noah change his mind? Talk about why it is good for people to take pride in the place where they live, work and play.
- Look at the wordless storyboard. Ask the children to talk about Noah's feelings as the story develops. What does Noah discover when he works with his friends to give his town a makeover? What have the children learned from this story?

Franklin Watts
First published in Great Britain in 2017 by The Watts Publishing Group

Credits
Series Editor: Sarah Peutrill
Series Designer: Cathryn Gilbert

ISBN 978 1 4451 5648 4

Printed in China

FSC
www.fsc.org

MIX
Paper from
responsible sources
FSC® C104740

Franklin Watts
An imprint of
Hachette Children's Group
Part of The Watts Publishing Group
Carmelite House
50 Victoria Embankment
London EC4Y 0DZ

An Hachette UK Company
www.hachette.co.uk

www.franklinwatts.co.uk